Epic Tales from

ADVENTURE TIME™

THE LONESOME OUTLAW

CARTOON NETWORK BOOKS
Penguin Young Readers Group
An Imprint of Penguin Random House LLC

Published in 2015 by Cartoon Network Books, an imprint of Penguin Random
House LLC, 345 Hudson Street, New York, New York 10014.
Printed in the USA.

Text written by Leigh Dragoon
Cover illustrated by Christopher Houghton

ISBN 978-0-8431-8310-8   10 9 8 7 6 5 4 3 2 1

Greetings, fans of epic adventure...

What you are holding in your hands is one of the most amazing novels in all of Ooo. These fantastical adventures by the master of awesome storytelling, T. T. MacDangereuse, are filled with tales of unimaginable heroism, perilous wonder, and unspeakable marvel. While some of these characters may seem familiar to you, keep in mind that nothing is what it seems when you enter the mind of T. T. MacDangereuse.

Epic Tales from

ADVENTURE TIME™

THE LONESOME OUTLAW

by T. T. MacDangereuse

An Imprint of Penguin Random House

CHAPTER 1

"What are you gonna spend your money on?" Marceline asked Bonnibel as they crawled through the chest-high grass. Her foster sister paused and scratched the side of her nose, her brow crinkling in concentration.

"Parts for the unipolar generator I'm building," she said. "Or a microscope. I haven't decided."

Marceline rolled her eyes. "Why can't you ever want something normal?"

"*Pfft*. You're one to talk." Cautiously, Bonnie sat up and pulled a wooden spyglass out of her duster's left-hand pocket. "You're happy with any ol' thing as long as it's red."

Marceline scowled and socked Bonnie lightly on the arm.

"Hey now," Bonnie murmured. "Careful." She steadied the spyglass.

Marceline tipped back her wide-brimmed straw hat. The hot noon sun beat down on them out of a cloudless sky, and the steady thrum of insects filled her ears. Wind swept across the prairie, passing through the tall grass stalks in waves.

"Do you see it?" Marceline asked. Her heart beat in her throat.

"Yeah," Bonnie said. "This is a perfect vantage point. They'll never see us coming."

And then, over the sound of the insects, over the rush of wind, they heard the train whistle. Both girls held their breath. Soon they'd know if their plan would work.

The train came around the curve of a hill. It was only four cars long, not counting the coal car.

"Well?" Marceline asked.

"They're stopping!" As the girls watched, the train shuddered to a halt, steam pouring from its smokestack, and two engineers hopped down from the engine. They moved forward, inspecting the tracks: the fallen tree, the damaged switch.

"Okay." Bonnie collapsed the spyglass and slipped it back into her coat. She pulled a pale blue bandanna out of her pocket. "Your turn."

Marceline squinted at the small pile of tinder she had placed at the base of the hill, a few yards from the tracks. For one terrible, sinking moment, she thought her unpredictable powers would fail her. Then a bright orange spark flared to life, and the tinder caught. The engineers started and turned as thick plumes of gray smoke rose from her fire. Marceline's fingers dug into dry soil knotted with grass roots as she channeled the smoke with her mind. It rolled toward the engineers, surrounding them like fog, turning their figures into flat silhouettes. Even up on the hill they could hear the men coughing. Suddenly, the men dropped to their bellies and began yelling and rolling across the ground.

Bonnie stood, fastening the bandanna tightly around her mouth and nose. Her eyes betrayed none of the frenetic excitement Marceline felt. When it came down to it, Bonnie was always deadly serious during a job. It was only afterward, when they were safe at home, that she allowed herself to joke and laugh.

Marceline tied her own bandanna, a triangle of scarlet fabric, around her face, and tightened her hat's stampede strings under her chin. "Just like we practiced. In and out, super fast!"

"Yep! Let's go."

They ran through the grass, slapping it aside impatiently, making a beeline for the last train car, their dusters flying out behind them. It was much easier this time for Marceline to keep one corner of her mind focused on the smoke, to hold it around the engineers. She felt a quick flush of pride. She was getting better, stronger.

There was no lock on the train car's door, which surprised her. The stagecoach they'd robbed three weeks ago had been locked down tighter than a gin-maker's cellar in teetotaler country. Still, why question good fortune? Marceline gripped the door handle and yanked it hard to the right. The heavy steel door slid smoothly on its tracks, revealing several large piles of wooden crates stamped with the logo of the National Treasury of Ooo. Bonnie hopped up into the car, pried the lid off the closest crate, and dug through the pale tangles of packing straw. She pulled free a small cloth bag, opened the drawstrings, and upended it. Perfect white pearls spilled into Bonnie's cupped hand. Marceline stared at them, enraptured. Just the thought of the amount of money they'd be able to get for even one of the pearls—it would pay for new farm equipment, the likes of which her foster dad had only ever dreamed of. It would buy cloth for her foster mom to make into new clothes. It would mean something besides sitting with an aching, empty belly during the dark, endless winter after a meager harvest.

"Here." Bonnie poured the pearls back into the pouch and shoved it into Marceline's hand. She dug out two more pouches and slipped them into her coat pockets. "All right, let's get out of here!"

They hopped down from the car, landing on their hands and knees, gravel crunching under their boots.

"You two, stop!"

Marceline whirled. A man, his face cast in deep shadow by his wide-brimmed hat, stood less than a dozen yards away. He held an object that looked suspiciously like a gun crossed with a croissant.

"Run!" Bonnie shouted, bolting toward the thick grass at the base of the hill. Cold fear shot through Marceline as she dashed after her.

WHUMP.

Marceline's mind registered the sound as a physical sensation, a percussive slap that knocked her off her feet. She sprawled across the ground, pebbles tearing at her palms, her hat tumbling off her head. She tried to call out to Bonnie, to tell her to wait, to help her, but she couldn't draw enough breath to shout. She tried to scramble to her feet, but her legs were limp and useless. To her horror, she realized she couldn't remember how to run. Her thoughts raced. What could she do? Gritting her teeth, she reached outward with her mind, grasping at the smoke rising from her now-blazing fire. If she could just drag it in between herself and the man, it might offer enough cover to allow her to escape.

But now, when she needed it the most, her power failed her. The smoke wouldn't obey her will. The wind caught it and swept it away harmlessly to the south.

"Roll over. Slowly."

Her mouth dry, Marceline did as she was told. The

man stood over her, his strange weapon pointed at her face. Even this close, the only facial feature she could make out was his mouth. It twisted as he spit a thin brown stream of tobacco juice into the grass. "Those engineers," he said, jerking a thumb over his shoulder, where the two men were shouting about aliens with candy clothes and mind-controlling ants. "They gonna be okay?"

She nodded, adopting as much false bravado as she could muster. "It's just panic-grass smoke. They'll be back to normal in a few minutes."

"Well, that's good. You're in enough trouble as it is." Holstering his weapon, the man reached up with a gloved hand and pushed his hat back on his head.

Marceline's stomach flipped. Ezra Sterling, the sheriff assigned to her hometown of Dustbowl City, population 600, glared down at her. She automatically reached for her bandanna to make sure it was still in place, hoping beyond hope that he wouldn't recognize her, that she might still have a chance to get away—

"I know it's you, Marceline. Ain't nobody else in ten counties got hair like yours. You wanna pick up your hat? Forehead's looking a wee bit pink."

She hadn't even noticed the unpleasant heat on the top of her head until he mentioned it. With trembling fingers, she snatched up her hat and put it on.

"All right. Let's get up now." Ezra grabbed her wrist and hauled her to her feet. Her legs wobbled. It took all her concentration to remain standing.

"Wh-what did you do to me?" she stammered.

"Nothing worse than what you did to them engineers." He patted his holster and smiled. "Just knocks the knowin' of how to run out of your head for a little while. Nothing permanent, so don't worry. That Bonnie with you?"

Marceline clamped her mouth shut, her heart pounding wildly. She wouldn't say anything. If there was even the slightest chance Bonnie could get away from here, get home, and claim ignorance of the whole hideous misadventure—

"Jasper!" Ezra shouted. "You got the other one?"

"Yes, sir."

Her whole body trembling, Marceline turned her head and saw the sheriff's son and deputy, Jasper Sterling, march a defeated, handcuffed Bonnie out of the tall grass. Dirt smudged her shirtfront, and her bandanna hung forlornly around her neck.

Ezra reached into Marceline's front pocket and retrieved the bag of pearls. "Well," he said. "Bonnibel Bubblegum. Fancy seeing you here. Though I suppose it ain't much of a surprise." He shook his head, unclipped his handcuffs, and slapped them around Marceline's wrists. "Your parents are gonna be mighty disappointed in the two of you."

CHAPTER 2

The air in the courthouse was stale, and sunlight fell in broad, mind-dullingly bright rectangles across the scarred floorboards. Marceline tried not to fidget as she and Bonnie stood before the bench, flanked by Ezra and Jasper, waiting for the traveling circuit judge to arrive. The townspeople had turned out in droves—every seat in the gallery was full. She supposed she couldn't blame them. Her and Bonnie's hijinks were the most interesting thing to happen in Dustbowl City in at least a hundred years.

A big greenbottle fly buzzed around the room in lazy loops. Marceline sighed and glanced at Ezra, who gazed stoically straight ahead. He and Jasper had barely spoken to them since they'd arrested her and Bonnie, though Bonnie's parents had visited them once in the jailhouse. They hadn't said much, and they hadn't wanted to speak to Marceline, which she supposed didn't really surprise her. She'd lived with the Bubblegums since age five, when her father had abandoned her, but she'd never really felt that comfortable with either Ma or Pa Bubblegum. They'd always treated her with a certain degree of wariness, as if she were a dog they were afraid might turn and bite them unexpectedly. At the jailhouse, they'd motioned Bonnie toward a corner of the cell and spoken to her in whispers. Then they left, without a glance at Marceline.

"What did they say?" she asked Bonnie.

Bonnie shook her head. She looked angry.

Now, in the pine-scented air of the courtroom, Marceline could feel her foster parents' stares burning into the back of her head. She'd spotted them as they slipped into the gallery. When she'd glanced at them, Ma Bubblegum had avoided her gaze.

Somewhere in the courthouse, a door slammed. A moment later the judge swept into the courtroom.

"All rise!" announced the bailiff, a large caramel apple, in a booming voice as Judge Ice King took his seat. He wore flowing blue robes and a huge black-and-white cowboy hat. Squinting down at her and Bonnie, he took off the hat and smacked it against the edge of the bench several times, knocking huge plumes of dust into the air.

"Ezra, Jasper." He nodded a greeting. "Let's get things under way, shall we? I read over your case file this morning and I've decided on my verdict."

Sudden cold shot down Marceline's spine. Was this all really happening so fast? Bonnie gripped her hand and squeezed it tightly.

"Miss Bubblegum." Judge Ice King's tone was

imperious. "I see no convincing evidence that you had any involvement in the crimes we're here to discuss today."

Every single person in the courtroom gasped. Marceline and Bonnie exchanged shocked glances.

"Your Honor!" shouted Sheriff Sterling. "She was there! We found two bags of pearls on her!"

"Pfft!" Judge Ice King waved his hand at Sterling dismissively. "It's just as likely she was out for a walk, found the pouches, and was apprehended by your son while she was approaching him to return them. Such a cute girl would never break the law."

"She *is* a very cute girl," the bailiff interjected.

Ezra's eyes looked like they were about to pop out of his head. His face had gone dead white, and now it began to turn the red of an overripe tomato. "Your Honor—" he began.

Judge Ice King glared down at him. "I've delivered my verdict, Sheriff. Don't give me any further reason

THE LONESOME OUTLAW   15

to question your investigative skills. Miss Bubblegum, you're free to go. Sheriff, remove her chains."

Stiff as a marionette, Ezra knelt and unlocked Bonnie's leg irons. With a happy cry, Ma and Pa Bubblegum dashed forward and wrapped Bonnie in a tight embrace. For the first time since they'd been caught, Marceline felt a surge of hope. Maybe Judge Ice King couldn't believe that two teenage girls could have pulled off a train heist.

"Miss Abadeer, step forward."

Marceline shuffled forward a few steps; her ankle chains clanked across the floor.

"Miss Abadeer," Judge Ice King boomed. "You ought to be ashamed of yourself! Not only did you rob a federal pearl shipment, you assaulted two engineers and endangered their lives by tampering with the train tracks. There's also evidence that you're an unrepentant criminal, responsible for a stagecoach raid and a whole spate of shoplifting. I hereby sentence you to four years of hard labor in the Joshua Tree Quarry."

Four years?! A dull buzz filled Marceline's head.

"Marceline!"

She turned to look back over her shoulder. Bonnie was reaching out to her, tears rolling down her cheeks. Ma and Pa Bubblegum were holding her back. Marceline met Ma's eyes. There was no kindness in them, just icy satisfaction.

The buzzing in her head grew louder and louder, until she could barely hear Judge Ice King's next words: "Sheriff Sterling, take her away."

White-hot rage washed over her, and hot sparks burst through the air around her. Ezra and Jasper cried out as they fell back.

"Sheriff!" Judge Ice King shot to his feet. "Control your prisoner!"

Marceline glared at Judge Ice King, and the tip of his long beard burst into flames. He shrieked, backpedaling. A quick-thinking root-beer float in the crowd sent a strawful of soda across the room and doused the fire in Judge Ice King's beard. People stampeded from the gallery as fires broke out throughout the courtroom. Then Ezra and Jasper tackled her.

"Get that collar on her!" Ezra shouted, sparks showering from the brim of his hat.

Something cold closed around her throat. Instantly, every fire in the courthouse died, leaving behind nothing but trails of white smoke.

They'd slapped a cold-iron collar on her neck. No magic known to man, woman, or Candy Person worked through cold iron. She hissed and spit as Ezra and Jasper hauled her to her feet.

"Well, I never!" Judge Ice King huffed.

CHAPTER 3

Marceline sat in her cell, alone except for a tiny snail crawling across the ceiling. She had no idea how much time had passed since she'd been sentenced. She could hear Ezra and Jasper arguing in the next room.

"Dad, this isn't right—we both know Bonnie was in on it."

"It is what it is, son. We're lawmen. There ain't nothin' more we can do about it except carry out the sentence. It ain't our place to question the judge."

CHAPTER 4

First thing the next morning, the Sterlings handcuffed Marceline, plopped a hat on her head, and led her out of the jail into the chilly predawn air. They tossed her up onto a horse's back, and Ezra clipped the chain between her handcuffs to an iron ring that had been drilled into the pommel of her horse's saddle. A brisk wind stroked her long hair, and a few stars glittered above the mountains to the east. Jasper was gloomy as he fastened her horse's lead onto his own horse's saddle.

"You up for doin' this on your own, son?" Ezra asked.

"We agreed. At least one of us needs to stay and watch over Dustbowl."

Ezra nodded. "All right, then." He and Jasper hugged.

"You don't give him any trouble, Marceline." Ezra wiped a few tears from his eyes as Jasper swung up into the saddle. Marceline sneered down at the man. Was he making fun of her? There wasn't anything she could do, not with her hands cuffed and the stupid collar around her neck.

At least not yet. She was confident she'd be able to figure something out between here and Joshua Tree.

Sutter Street, the main road out of town, was deserted, probably due to how early it was, but Marceline still felt a sting of rejection, disappointment that no one had come to see her off. She was going to disappear from the lives of everyone she'd ever known, and it was almost like it had already happened.

The wind picked up, pushing hard against her back, as if it, too, were hurrying her out of town.

Marceline scowled. All she wanted was to forget

about Dustbowl City and Ma and Pa Bubblegum and even Bonnie as quickly as possible.

Jasper twisted in the saddle to look back at her. "Y'know, you didn't do yourself any favors yesterday. Judge Ice King was so angry, he resentenced you to five years instead of four."

Marceline shrugged.

"How long have you been able to do that fire thing, anyway? I don't remember you being able to do that back in grammar school."

"Yeah, well, back then you were a scrawny, nerdly little dork with buckteeth. We've all changed."

Jasper sighed and turned back around.

It didn't stay cold for long. As the sun cleared the mountains, she began to sweat. Despite her best intentions to stay sharp and keep her eyes peeled for an opportunity to escape, as the day wore on, Marceline sank into a stupor. She was hot and sweaty and miserable, her mouth tasted like dust, and her heart felt squashed. She barely noticed when Jasper reined in his horse. Blinking, she stared at their surroundings. They stood alongside a thick copse of cottonwood trees. Over the gentle rustling of leaves, she could just make out the gurgle of water running across stones.

"We'll eat some lunch here. Wait out the hottest part of the day." Jasper's voice was flat. He slung a satchel over his shoulder, unhooked Marceline's handcuffs from the pommel, and helped her dismount. Pebbles ground into her feet through the thin soles of her nearly worn-out boots. Keeping one hand on her shoulder at all times, Jasper led her into the wonderfully cool shade beneath the trees. They sat on a pair of smooth boulders dappled with leaf shadows. The horses made straight for the little brook that cut across the center of the grove and dipped their velvety muzzles into the water.

"Here." Jasper pulled a sandwich wrapped in wax

paper from his satchel and pressed it into her hands.

"Could you take these off?" Marceline shook her hands, jingling the handcuff chain. "It's not like I can use my powers even if you take 'em off."

"No, I'm sorry, I can't," Jasper said. He met her gaze, and one corner of his mouth quirked into a smile. "My dad would turn me upside down and use my head as a mop to muck out the cells."

Laughter burst out of Marceline's mouth, surprising her almost as much as it appeared to surprise Jasper. He began to laugh, too, and the laughter built in both their throats, growing into great, belly-shaking guffaws. Their chuckles slowly faded. Marceline wiped at her eyes, her stomach aching. It felt good to laugh, to have something to laugh about. For a long moment she and Jasper stared at each other, and Marceline felt like a normal person again. Then Jasper sighed, and the levity seemed to go out of him in a rush, leaving his face solemn. He eyed her sadly before glancing away. "I'm sorry about this," he said. "It's not right, it's not fair . . ."

He shook his head and pushed himself to his feet. "Eat up." As she unwrapped the sandwich and crammed it into her mouth, he strode to the brook, knelt, and refilled his canteen.

"How much farther we gotta go?" she asked around a mouthful of lettuce, steak, and chickpeas.

Jasper shrugged and set the canteen next to Marceline's leg.

"Maybe another two days," he said. "Depends if the weather holds."

Marceline rolled her eyes. Wildfires, swarms of locusts, broilingly hot summer days, torrential thunderstorms, ice storms, fog storms—everyone in Dustbowl City had seen it all. She'd be more surprised if the weather *didn't* change. She wadded the wax paper into a ball and tossed it against the nearest tree trunk.

Jasper heaved a ginormous sigh and massaged his temples.

"You got a problem?" Marceline asked.

Jasper picked up the wax-paper ball and stuffed it into his knapsack. "You really shouldn't do that," he muttered.

"Really? I'm about to serve a five-year sentence in a rock quarry, and you're going to give me guff about littering?"

Jasper's whole face turned stink-fly scarlet. "Well, when you put it that way, it sounds ridiculous."

Marceline rolled her eyes again. "You're wound way too tight." She took a swig from the canteen. "You got anything else in that bag? I'm still hungry."

Jasper pulled out a purplish-black apple and handed it to her. He sat and watched while she ate it, his face strangely blank. Marceline ate as noisily and messily as possible, hoping it bothered Jasper. What had being good and polite ever gotten her? It hadn't been enough to earn Ma and Pa Bubblegum's love. Well, truth be told, being bad hadn't worked out so well for her, either, but still . . . Apple juice dripping down her chin, she sucked out the pips, spit them over her shoulder, and tossed away the core. With a sigh, she wiped her chin off on the shoulder of her shirt.

"Well?" she asked. "Shouldn't we get going?"

"Yeah. I suppose." Jasper stood and turned away from her, staring off into the distance. A few palm-sized cottonwood leaves brushed gently against his cheek. When he turned back, something in his eyes had changed.

"What?" she snapped.

Jasper reached into his shirt pocket and pulled out two small keys knotted onto a thin leather cord. Without a word, he unlocked her handcuffs and the magic-suppressing collar.

Marceline blinked in disbelief. "What are you doing?"

Jasper backed away slowly, clucking his tongue to call the horses, who lifted their heads and walked to his side. He gathered up the reins and pulled himself into the saddle with a single smooth motion. "I'll see you around, Marceline." He nodded at her and tipped his hat.

Then he was gone.

CHAPTER 5

Marceline sat on the boulder, frozen in shock. Was this some kind of trick? Finally, when the sound of the horses' hooves had faded, she stood. Moving slowly, her senses strained to their limits, she inched out of the grove, expecting at any point to be tackled by an irate law officer. Nothing. There was nobody there. Jasper had really left.

The strength went out of her legs, and she collapsed. She was free. Free!

A small, obnoxiously insistent voice in the back of her mind spoke up. *Free to go where, to do what?* She couldn't go home. Not only would no one (except *maaaaaybe* Bonnie) be happy to see her, she'd get Jasper in trouble, and that was a poor way to repay the young man for his kindness.

"It doesn't matter," she whispered. She'd heard it was a bad sign when a person started talking to herself, but it wasn't as if there were anyone around she had to worry about impressing. "Just get out of here! You can figure everything out later."

Marceline knotted her hat's stampede strings tightly under her chin and ducked back into the grove. She couldn't just run off willy-nilly. She needed to be smart. Her gaze fell on the canteen Jasper had given her. There! That was something! She snatched it up and tied it onto her belt.

The stream. I should follow the stream.

Yes. That was as good a plan as any. The stream ran west, away from Dustbowl City. If she followed it, she'd stand a decent chance of finding food, as in her experience, berry bushes tended to grow thickly around any water source. And she wouldn't have to worry about dying of thirst, which was good, because she'd heard that was a horrible way to go.

Her heart beating wildly, Marceline set off, being careful to step on rocks whenever possible to avoid leaving tracks. There was no sense in making things easy for Jasper on the off chance he changed his mind and tried to recapture her.

Once out from beneath the trees, the stream followed a twisting path. The banks rose on either side, first to shoulder height, then over her head, cutting off her view of the surrounding terrain. She felt more at ease; sure, she wouldn't get much warning if someone tried to sneak up on her, but at least she was equally well hidden.

The day grew hotter. She took off her duster and knotted it around her waist. The ground changed from well-packed sand to rocks and pebbles. She was careful to plant each foot firmly on the shifting gravel. The last thing she needed was to twist—or even break—her ankle.

As she moved deeper into the gully, the bank grew narrower. Just when she thought she was going to have to pull off her boots and wade through the cold water, she came around a turn, and the landscape opened before her. The stream fanned out into a wide braided delta across sand so white that for a moment she thought it was actually snow. The air shimmered with heat. She stood on the shore of a dry lake, what Pa Bubblegum had called a *playa*.

Marceline frowned, trying to decide what to do. She hadn't put as much ground between herself and Dustbowl City as she would have liked. But heading out into the sun-drenched hardpan during the hottest part of the day wasn't a smart move. Reluctantly, she squatted in the shade of the gully wall, tipped her hat brim down over her face, and tried to sleep.

CHAPTER 6

Marceline started awake with no clear idea of what had disturbed her. She pushed back her hat and lurched to her feet. She was alone. The air had cooled, and the breeze had dried the sweat stains on her shirt. Directly ahead, the sun shone into her eyes as it sank toward the horizon.

The palm of her left hand stung, a single drop of blood welling from a small scratch near the base of her thumb. She frowned and wiped her hand on her pants. "What the cabbage?" she muttered, and took a swig from her canteen. The tepid water tasted flat and metallic. On the far side of the hardpan, she could just make out a jagged line of mountains, thrown into sharp relief by the setting sun. Before she could begin to second-guess herself, she refilled the canteen in one of the clear rivulets, clipped it back onto her belt, and started out across the hardpan.

For the first few miles she sang to herself, nonsense about flowers and flour and roses and rosacea and felines and fungus. Then her mouth and throat became too dry, and she fell silent. The sky turned a deep cherry red. She stopped for a few minutes to rest, heaving a sigh. The mountains appeared no closer, but in the fading light, she could pick out a mound of boulders off to her right, dotted with the feathery silhouettes of trees. It didn't look too far away. Trees meant good odds there'd be a spring. Her head canted at an awkward angle so her hat could block the sun's rays, she trudged onward.

Halfway there, Marceline cried out as a sharp pain flared on the back of her neck. Snarling, she slapped her hand against the spot. Was it a mosquito, a horsefly?

There was a burst of high-pitched laughter right beside her ear. Marceline whirled. Nothing.

Another stinging bite, this time on the back of her hand. She cried out, more from fear than pain. Once again that same disembodied, chilling laugh. This time, when she snapped her head around, she saw something. A smear of dust-colored haze, like a tattered scrap of gauze. The hint of features: beady black eyes and a red mouth glittering with jagged white teeth.

A sand demon. Almost as soon as she spotted it, it sank into the ground.

Marceline's stomach flipped. "Oh my glob!" Ma and Pa Bubblegum had ordered her to never take Glob's name in vain, but if there had ever existed a situation that called for casual swearing, this was it. Most of Dustbowl City's children were taught to fear sand demons from an early age, but Ma and Pa Bubblegum had told her and Bonnie over and over again that the tales were nothing more than rank superstition, and they wouldn't brook raising children who believed such nonsense.

Fat lot they knew.

"If you let us have all your blood, we'll be your best best friends." One of the demons had materialized right in front of her face. Its voice was nerve-rackingly high-pitched.

"Yes," said another, appearing beside the first. "Best best."

She made a break for it, sand gritting under her feet, racing for the island of boulders, frantically dredging up every scrap of anti-sand-demon wisdom she'd absorbed over the years. If she was very, very lucky, she might make it to the boulders and could huddle under her duster. Any kind of sand monster would be able to come up through the hardpan to get at her, and they grew more powerful after dark, but they couldn't go through rock, and their teeth, though sharp, weren't supposed to be particularly long. Hopefully they wouldn't be able to bite through her duster's thick fabric.

Now that they had her running scared, the demons weren't as subtle. They bit at any exposed skin they could find. She waved her arms frantically, but there was nothing to the demons; her hands passed through them as if they were wisps of cloud. More and more of them gathered around her, filling the air with their nails-on-a-chalkboard laughter.

Ragged, waist-high brush encircled the mound of boulders, and Marceline hit it at full speed, twigs crunching underfoot. Only then, when it was too late to back out, did she realize the bushes were covered in tiny thorns that snagged at her clothing and skin. She howled, beating at the slender branches with her hands, struggling to force her way through. With one final, desperate lurch, she tore herself free and scrambled up the side of the nearest boulder. The light was fading quickly, and the demons' laughter grew louder and louder. Her hands scrabbled at the jagged granite, finding holds. As soon as she dragged herself up on top of the outcrop, she reached for her duster—

It was gone. She rolled onto her back, looked down, and spotted it tangled in the brush ten feet below her perch. The sand demons hovered above it, grinning, saliva dripping from their lips. Taunting her.

Pure rage poured through Marceline's body, drowning her fear. She lashed out with her power, and the brush burst into flames. Most of the sand demons screamed and disappeared, but a few zipped around the fire and came at her. Marceline leaped backward.

A splintering crack was the only warning she had before the ground dropped out from under her.

CHAPTER 7

She fell for what felt like an eternity into pure darkness. Her terror was complete, overwhelming. She couldn't think, couldn't scream—there wasn't time for anything.

She smacked down hard against a solid surface and shot forward at a sloped, downward angle. She flung out her arms, trying to slow herself down, but her hands slapped against walls as smooth as glass. She slid on and on, picking up speed as she went.

Just when she'd started to think she was going to slide forever, a pale white circle appeared in front of her. It grew larger and then she shot out of it, sailed through the air—*Oh great*, she thought bitterly, *more falling*—and, with a huge splash, flopped into a pool of surprisingly warm water.

She struggled to the surface, gasped, and shook her ringing head, treading water while she took in her surroundings. Sheer rock walls surrounded her, and the moon shone overhead. Directly ahead was a strip of sand, and she paddled over to it. As soon as her feet were able to touch the bottom, she staggered out of the pool and collapsed, gasping, on the shore.

"You are awesome!"

Marceline's muscles trembled with exhaustion as she pushed herself up. A small, mint-green automaton, like something out of one of Bonnie's futuristic magazines, toddled toward her on pipe-cleaner legs, waving equally skinny arms.

Marceline groaned. She was done. If this thing wanted to eat her or squash her or use her skull as a planter pot, that was just fine with her. She didn't have the strength to put up any kind of a fight.

"You are the best thief ever!" the thing said in a pleasant, lightly accented voice. "So strong! So handsome! So quick and intelligent!"

Marceline flipped her sopping hair out of her eyes. "Who are you?"

"I am BMO! You look hungry. Here." There was a sharp popping sound, and the tiny automaton handed Marceline a piece of nicely browned toast.

It could be poisoned. Or drugged. Marceline, suddenly aware that she was starving, didn't care. She crammed it into her mouth.

"Thank you, BMO." Crumbs sprayed out of her mouth. "What are you doing here?"

"You left me here, you silly! I'm your best friend, most loyal companion, and most devoted personal self-esteem manager." BMO peered at her. "Though you do look different from the last time I saw you. You're not so tall . . . or bearded . . . or male. But that's okay. I love you no matter how much you change. It has been a very long time since you used the super-fun escape tunnel slide."

BMO wrapped tiny, gentle hands around Marceline's biceps. Slowly, she managed to get her feet and legs under her in the correct order.

"Come," BMO said. "This way."

She followed it into a narrow, moonlit slickrock canyon. The twists and turns soon completely befuddled her. Just when she thought she couldn't stagger another step, BMO led her into a huge cave lit with a soft green phosphorescence that shone from the rocks themselves.

Marceline stared in utter shock. The cave was so well-appointed and opulent, it looked like a picture she'd seen in a magazine. Plush carpets covered the floor, and beautiful paintings hung from the walls.

"Come, come, I've got everything waiting for you." BMO led her to an overstuffed chair set before a clay chiminea filled with glowing coals. She sank into the cushions while BMO disappeared into another part of the cave.

When it returned, it was carrying a huge dinner plate full of food. Marceline's belly growled like a pack of wolves as soon as the smell reached her, and she didn't even wait to take the silverware BMO offered her, just started cramming the food into her mouth as soon as it handed her the plate. Mashed potatoes dripping with fresh butter, a thick juicy steak, a baked apple stuffed with oatmeal and raisins. She'd never had such good food. Even in better years, when the weather had been clement and the crops rich, Ma and Pa Bubblegum had been forced to sell most of their produce. Nearly every meal they'd shared over the years had been some wretched combination of grits, green beans, roasted cactus pads, and the sickly sweet fruit from the fields.

BMO whisked the plate away as soon as she

finished. "Here." It nudged her elbow. It held a blue mug filled with a steaming dark brown liquid that smelled like nothing she'd ever had. She took a sip. It was sweet and rich and creamy.

"Nothing like hot cocoa after a hard day's work, Billy." BMO frowned. "Or has your name changed, as well?"

"Marceline. Call me Marceline."

"Excellent. Would you like your evening read now, Marceline?"

"Sure."

BMO pulled a thick notebook from seemingly nowhere and tossed it onto Marceline's lap, where it fell open to a dog-eared page.

I AM KIND! I AM A GOOD PERSON! I WILL CREATE

MY OWN FUTURE!

"Um . . . BMO, what is this, again?"

"Silly! It's your daily affirmations journal, of course."

Now that she'd had time to look more closely at her surroundings, Marceline noticed scraps of paper pasted to nearly every surface, bearing similar messages. Her eyes widened. Whoever this Billy guy was, he had one heck of a self-esteem problem.

"How long has it been since I've been here?" she asked.

"It's been five and a half years, but as you can see, I've done an excellent job maintaining your super-secret hideout. I dust every morning, and water the cacti in the cacti garden, and sweep—"

"That's great, BMO, just great." If it had been that long since Billy had put in an appearance, she doubted he was going to show up any time soon. She might as well enjoy his things. It'd be a shame to let them go to waste. "Everything looks wonderful." She handed BMO back the journal. "I think I've had enough . . . ah . . . affirming for the day."

"Maybe now you would like to play your music,

yes?" BMO whisked away the journal and, moments later, pressed a guitar into her hands.

"Oh, I don't think I can play," Marceline said.

"*Ah-hah-hah!* You silly! Of course you can play." BMO's face abruptly darkened. "If you couldn't, I'd start to suspect perhaps you are not you, and then things would become very messy indeed."

Marceline swallowed hard. "Maybe I should take a little time to tune it—"

"It's perfectly tuned! I take care of everything. I am a most devoted friend. Now play."

Marceline settled the fingers of her left hand on the guitar's neck and strummed tentatively with her right. As soon as her fingertips touched the metal strings, something strange happened. It was as if electricity shot up her arm and into her brain, where it formed a nest full of gummiflies and birds and music notes and words, and when she opened her mouth, beautiful, soulful music poured out.

Her fingers moved confidently over the strings as if she'd played every day of her life. The song she sang perfectly expressed the range of emotions she'd felt over the course of the day. She broke off and stared down at the guitar in shock.

BMO sighed. "Best magic guitar ever."

CHAPTER 8

Five Years Later . . .

Marceline finished singing and sat motionless, waiting for the final notes to fade. For a moment, a perfect hush fell over the crowded saloon, then the spectators burst into wild applause. Marceline smiled, stood, and swept off her wide-brimmed hat in the theatrical gesture that had become her trademark.

"The Saltsea Bard!" the saloon owner shouted as she glided off the stage. She was filled with the giddiness she always felt after a successful show.

"What a wonderful performance!" BMO enthused as she stepped into the closet the saloon's owner had set aside for her to use as a changing room. She grinned as she handed BMO the guitar. As she shook her hair out of the tight braid she kept it in while she played, BMO placed the guitar carefully in its black, velvet-lined case.

"I know! Did you see how many people are out there?" She sat on the stool set in front of a cracked mirror and began wiping the stage makeup off her face. "At least twice as many as last time."

"Here." BMO tapped a thick brown envelope against her thigh. "While you were onstage, a letter came for you."

Marceline turned the envelope over in her hands. As large as it was, it was very light. More fan mail? The return address read: *B. Bubblegum, 10 Sutter Street, Dustbowl City.*

A chill pierced her heart. In the years since her conviction, she'd done her best to avoid Dustbowl and everyone she'd ever known there, both physically and mentally. BMO, who acted as her manager, was always very careful to schedule performances as far away from her birthplace as possible. She'd been careful to stay hundreds of miles away, performing in the cities and towns lining the shore of the vast Salt Sea, a formidable expanse of coastline where pink-salt waves whispered across the rocky shores.

And now this letter. Why? Why now? Her stomach churned as she turned the envelope over and over in her hands. She supposed she couldn't really claim to be surprised. As her fame grew, and word of her amazing performances spread, she'd known that someday someone from her past might hear about her. But so much time had passed, she'd grown complacent.

Her hands clenched the envelope, wrinkling it. She almost told BMO to throw it away. Then, as if they had a mind of their own, her fingers ripped it open, and she pulled out the sheet of doubled-over paper inside.

Dear Marceline, the letter began, written in Bonnie's familiar sloppy script.

> *Or should I call you the Saltsea Bard?*
> *I'm so glad to hear of your success.*
> *I know this letter must come as a surprise*
> *(I hope not an unpleasant one), but you're never*
> *far from my thoughts. I miss you terribly. I'm*
> *writing this letter to beg you to consider visiting*
> *Dustbowl City. Things have changed here. The*
> *old sheriff, Ezra Sterling, retired a long time ago.*
> *His son, Jasper, is in charge now. Please, please*
> *come home, if only for a few days.*
> *Love,*
> *Bonnie*

"What is wrong?" BMO asked.

It was only then that Marceline realized she was crying. She wiped her eyes with the back of her hand.

She felt frightened and heartbroken and rejected and happy all at once, and it was terribly confusing. As much as she'd tried to deny it, a part of herself—a big part—missed her home, missed Bonnie, even missed Ma and Pa Bubblegum.

BMO stood on its tippy toes, trying to see what the letter said. "Is it bad news?"

"No." Marceline stared at the letter, reading the words over and over again. "Not—not really." She fell silent and waited for her thoughts to settle. "BMO," she said finally, "I have a lot of money, don't I?"

BMO smiled. "You sure do! Fifty-four thousand, six hundred and twenty-two dollars, to be precise." BMO took its managerial duties very seriously and was an excellent accountant.

Marceline nodded. She had more money than she'd ever dreamed possible, money that was hers, that she had earned with her voice and the aid of the magic guitar. Anyway, it had been five years: the term of her sentence. As far as anyone would know, she'd served her time and been released. She doubted Jasper was going to say anything—he had as much reason to hide the truth as she did. Not to mention, she wasn't as naive as she'd once been. She knew how the world worked. If she went home and anyone gave her trouble, she could bribe them easily.

Marceline slipped the letter into the pocket of her fitted maroon waistcoat. "BMO, find out what it'll take to schedule a concert in Dustbowl City."

CHAPTER 9

One more than when she'd been a resident. Below the neatly painted signpost, someone had pasted a poster that announced the date of her concert. It bore a very good likeness of her standing in a dramatic pose, playing her guitar and singing.

BMO peered around her from its position on the travel pack she'd lashed behind her horse's saddle. "Princess Allegri did a wonderful job with the graphic design."

Marceline nodded and kneed her horse forward. She couldn't help feeling a little nervous as she and

BMO rode down Sutter Street, but she kept her spine straight and her head tilted back, projecting confidence and pride. She'd been careful to time her arrival close to sunset, when most people would be home eating dinner. She didn't need to ask BMO where they were staying for the duration of the trip. Dustbowl City had only one hotel, the Old Town Hotel. She didn't know why they called it the "Old Town." All of Dustbowl was old. She found her way easily; almost nothing appeared to have changed. Things only looked a bit smaller, a bit more run-down in the deepening twilight. The hotel's facade looked exactly as she remembered: a two-story wooden building painted a nice shade of teal with white trim. Lights shone in the front windows and one of the upstairs rooms. A stableboy stepped forward and took her horse's reins as soon as she slid down from its sweaty back. The boy waited patiently while she grabbed her bags, shouldered her guitar, and helped BMO down, before leading the horse off toward the stables.

A bell above the door tinkled as Marceline let herself into the hotel's plain, sparsely decorated lobby. A woman with pink hair piled up on top of her head in a messy bun stood behind the front desk, writing something in a thick ledger by the light of a kerosene lamp. She looked up at Marceline, pushing a pair of wire-rimmed spectacles higher up on her pert nose.

It was Bonnie. Marceline recognized her immediately, and by the look on the other young woman's face, she knew she had been recognized, as well. Marceline opened her mouth, not sure what was going to come out—

And Bonnie raced around the desk and wrapped Marceline in a tight hug.

"Oh, Marcy! You came!" she whispered. "You really came!"

Tears filled Marceline's eyes. "I missed you, too."

"Ahem," BMO said politely.

Marceline took a step back. "This is my manager, BMO."

"It's nice to meet you." Bonnie took Marceline's hand and led her into a small office just behind the front desk. "Come into the back, I'll fix some hot tea and biscuits. You can leave your things on the counter. The bellhop'll take them up to your room. I saved you the Presidential Suite, of course."

"I'll wait out here," BMO said. "You two catch up."

Marceline set her bags down where Bonnie indicated, though she kept her guitar with her. "How long have you worked here?"

"For a few years. The owner lets me have a room for free." She gestured to a pair of cane-backed chairs next to a small table as she set out two teacups, a dark green teapot, and a plate covered with a clean towel. She glanced away and busied herself with the tea. "Marceline, about the trial—"

Marceline sat in one of the chairs. "I don't want

to talk about it. It's in the past. Let it stay there."

Some emotion she couldn't name passed through Bonnie's eyes, then the girl smiled and poured tea into the cups. The warm, homey smell of cinnamon filled the small room. "I'm so excited about your concert!" she said. "Your life must be so exciting."

"I can't complain." Marceline sipped her tea. "How have you been?"

Bonnie quirked a smile. "I can't complain." Then the smile slipped from her face, and she sat and picked up her teacup. "You know what it's like here. Nothing much changes. Everyone remembers everything." Her eyes grew distant. "I'm not on terribly good terms with Ma and Pa right now. They don't approve of me moving out, but . . . well, I felt it was time."

"Not on good terms, huh? But they were always so easy to get along with," she said, rolling her eyes. Bonnie smiled weakly. There was a brief silence as Marceline remembered the fiery look Ma had given her during the trial, the way she and Pa had turned their backs on her. "How are they?" she finally asked grudgingly.

"They're fine."

"Do they ever talk about me?" The words surprised Marceline as soon as she spoke them, and she was even more surprised at how badly she wanted Bonnie to say yes, they cared about her, missed her—

Bonnie's cheeks flushed. "I think they still have a lot of hard feelings. I've tried talking to them about it, told them I was as much to blame as you . . . but you remember how stubborn they are."

A hard lump lodged in Marceline's throat. She set down her teacup and stood. "I . . . I think I need to step out for some air."

"Oh, you must be exhausted." Bonnie stood. "I'll make sure your room is ready."

Marceline nodded and hurried out. BMO glanced up at her questioningly as she swept past.

Outside, it had grown completely dark. There was no moon, and a chill wind blew leaves and small tumbleweeds down the street. Marceline shivered and rubbed her arms. She hadn't realized how much Ma and Pa Bubblegum's rejection would hurt. However they felt about her now, they had been her parents, too, for a very long time. She sighed and gave the doorjamb a hard, angry kick. Maybe she shouldn't have come back.

But then I would have wondered. At least now I know.

And she was glad to see Bonnie again. At least the connection they had once shared was still strong, if a bit rusted by time.

As she turned to go back inside, the hairs on the back of her neck went up. Someone was watching her.

Trying to appear casual, she turned, pretending to examine a loose thread on her shirt, and quickly scanned the street.

In the shadows of a building twenty or thirty feet away stood a short, tan dog wearing a large cowboy hat, and a young teen boy with pale blond hair. He bore a long, sheathed sword on his back. Silver stars, marking them as deputies, glinted on their chests. As soon as they realized she had spotted them, the deputies put their heads together and whispered fiercely back and forth. Then the dog nodded decisively and marched across the street, heading straight toward her. The teenager hung back, watching the dog in dismay, before he jogged after him and caught up.

"Marceline Abadeer?" the dog said.

Marceline's heart skipped a beat, but she kept her composure. She'd expected to be confronted by someone sooner or later. So what if it was sooner? She was ready. "Can I help you?" She slipped a hand into her pocket, where she'd tucked an envelope full of crisp hundred-dollar bills.

Both deputies stopped at the bottom of the

porch steps. The dog crossed his arms over his chest and glared up at her. His partner looked nervous. "I'm Deputy Jake the Dog, and this is Deputy Finn the Human."

Marceline stared at him levelly. "And?"

Deputy Jake elbowed Deputy Finn hard in the ribs. "We're keeping an eye on you!" Finn exclaimed, lunging forward to shake a fist in her face. His eyes bulged. He leaped back to his place beside his partner.

"I may have been just a young pup during your trial, but I heard all about you and your crimes, and you better be planning on walking a real fine line while you're back in town," Jake said, staring at her through slitted eyes.

Marceline heaved a sigh. "I don't want any trouble. I'm just here for my concert."

"Oh, and you just *happen* to be staying at the hotel managed by your former partner-in-crime?"

She rolled her eyes. "It's the only hotel in town."

"Well, still . . ." Jake nudged Finn again.

"HOOOHAAAAHH!!!" Finn shouted, executing an impressive, if somewhat unconventional, forearm block. "Shmow-tow! We're super tough! Save your arguments for someone who cares, foul varmint!" Veins bulged in his cherry-red face.

"Okay, that's probably enough. Calm down," Jake said quickly, before turning back to Marceline. "What he said! Anyway, you're not fooling anyone. I've been doing this a long time, and if I know anything, it's that once a criminal, always a criminal. Don't be thinking that 'cause you served your time, you're not on my radar. You and Bonnibel."

Marceline's temper flared. "She was acquitted. Leave her out of this."

Jake snorted. "Maybe so, but not everyone 'round these here parts agrees with Judge Ice King's verdict." He backed away, one slow, deliberate step at a time.

"Our eyes. On you," Finn said, pointing first at

his eyes with the two forefingers on his right hand, then jabbing his fingers in her direction.

When she was sure they'd actually gone, Marceline blew her bangs out of her eyes and sagged back against the hotel's front door. She was exhausted, emotionally and physically. All she wanted was to collapse into a nice, warm bed.

CHAPTER 10

The next morning, when Marceline stepped out
of her room, she noticed that BMO had tacked a note
to her door: *At the concert hall. Meet me there.* She
sighed. BMO was never one to shirk from its duties.
Still, there was something to be said for enjoying
a relaxing morning, maybe a nice brunch . . . She
headed downstairs. "Concert hall" was a nice way
to describe Dustbowl's sad clapboard theater, which
usually hosted community productions of musicals
and four-hundred-year-old plays.

Downstairs, Bonnie stood behind the counter
talking to a tall dark-haired man. As Marceline came

down the steps, the man turned, and she realized it was Jasper. He looked much as she remembered, with the same flinty gray-green eyes and tousled brown hair, though he'd grown taller and filled out. There was one major difference: a silver sheriff's star was pinned to his gray vest's lapel.

"Jasper," she blurted. She couldn't keep the surprise out of her voice.

Bonnie smiled. "See, I told you she'd remember you. We were just talking about how much we're looking forward to your concert tonight."

"Yeah," Marceline said, suddenly nervous. Her hand wanted very badly to go back to the envelope of money in her front pocket, but instead she slapped her hat on her head and tried to look tough. "Sorry I can't stick around for this lovely little reunion. BMO's waiting for me at the theater."

"Oh!" Bonnie said. "Do you want some tea or sandwiches or something to take with you?"

"No, I'm fine!" Keeping her head high, Marceline hurried across the room.

Out front, Deputies Jake and Finn sat on folding lawn chairs directly across the street from the hotel, sharing a huge bag of popcorn. "We're watching you!" Finn shouted. Pieces of popcorn flew from his mouth, and he must have inhaled one, because he bent over in a harsh coughing fit. Jake pounded him on the back. More popcorn crumbs spewed across the street.

"Hey, wait up a sec," Jasper said, coming up behind her.

"Our sheriff's on to you, too!" Jake shouted between whacks.

Marceline folded her arms. It took little effort to lodge another popcorn kernel in Finn's throat with her power. "What do you want?" she asked Jasper.

Jasper rubbed the back of his neck. "I'd like to apologize for my deputies. Deputy the Dog is a little . . . opinionated."

She quirked an eyebrow, pointedly ignoring the drama on the other side of the street as Finn hawked up an impressive popcorn loogie. "And Deputy the Human?"

"He's a little . . . excitable."

Marceline rolled her eyes. "They new in town? I don't remember them."

"Just moved here two years ago." He shrugged and spread his hands helplessly. "They want to make their mark. Don't worry, I'll convince them to turn it down a bit."

"Well, thanks, I guess," she drawled. "I gotta be somewhere. So long."

As she turned to go, Jasper caught her hand. "Marceline, wait." His voice was soft, and he met her gaze directly. His face was open and honest. "I want you to know, as far as the record's concerned, you served your time. I made sure of it."

She didn't know what to say. To her horror, she

felt blood rush into her cheeks. She hated feeling out of control, and this whole scene definitely qualified.

"Thanks," she snapped, jerking her hand out of his grip. "I appreciate it. But that doesn't mean I owe you anything, and it doesn't make you my *lurve* interest. See ya around."

She turned and marched off up the street, heading toward the theater, and despite the fact that she kind of wanted to, she refused to turn around and see what kind of look Jasper had on his face.

CHAPTER 11

BMO was reading information off its own screen with a mirror when Marceline arrived at the theater. BMO glanced up at her and smiled as she stalked across the wooden stage toward it.

"What's the matter?" BMO asked. "Your face is all red. Your eyes are really buggy, too."

"Nothing. I'm fine," she snapped, and threw herself into a canvas chair.

"Oh, okay." BMO hummed tunelessly as it began performing sound checks. "I'll remember that you being fine includes your regular face and also that one."

CHAPTER 12

Marceline sat cross-legged on the bed in her hotel room and tuned her guitar.

She knew there were some performers who got gummiflies before a performance, but Marceline had never been one of them. She loved being onstage. When she sang, and everyone's attention was focused on her, she felt powerful, in control. The only thing she liked better was now, the time right before a concert, when she had this span of quiet time to herself.

The G string was a little flat. Even a magic instrument needed maintenance. Marceline turned the peg carefully. Since music had become her livelihood, she'd taken the time to learn how to play a regular guitar, and how to read sheet music and compose. After all, what if someday the magical guitar were stolen or broken or lost? She'd purchased a non-magical guitar, which she often played at smaller venues. Still . . . it couldn't compare to the magic guitar. When she played it, it felt like the instrument and her mind and her voice and her soul were all connected.

Her pointed ears abruptly pricked at the scrape of a boot heel in the hall right outside her door. She set the guitar down on the bed and crept to the door. She knew Bonnie had gone out to have dinner at her parents'—not that Marceline was bitter about not being invited or anything—and BMO was at the theater, finishing the setup.

Contorting her features in the scariest expression she was capable of, Marceline wrenched open the door and lunged out into the hall.

No one was there, but something crunched under her foot. She glanced down. Her left boot was stamped firmly on top of a tissue-paper-wrapped bouquet of pink and purple desert posies. She lifted her foot. A white card, now smudged by her boot print, read: *Good luck tonight—Jasper.*

She caught him halfway down the stairs. "Jasper—" she said, then fell silent, frozen at the top of the staircase, tongue-tied yet again.

He looked up at her shamefacedly. "I . . . I want you to know, I don't expect anything from you."

Now she was the one who felt ashamed, because she believed him. She dropped her gaze. "I'm sorry I was so sharp with you earlier. I guess I didn't know what to expect when I came back here. I kind of expected the worst."

Jasper offered her a warm, lopsided smile. "I don't blame you." He tipped his hat at her, a gentlemanly gesture she associated with his father. "Ma'am," he said, affecting a thick drawl. Marceline laughed.

"Jasper, hang on a sec." She ran back to her room, grabbed a card out of her bag, and dashed back to the stairs. "Here." She handed him the card. "It's a backstage pass. I gave one to Bonnie, too," she said quickly, determined to play it cool. "Maybe we can hang out after the concert. Catch up."

Jasper's smile widened. "Sure thing," he said.

CHAPTER 13

Marceline stood in the center of the stage and stared out into the packed theater. Most everyone she'd grown up around was out there, watching her. She struck a dramatic pose and nodded to BMO, who snapped on the spotlight and trained it on her. The audience disappeared in a blaze of white light. Marceline swept her arm down over the strings, and a power chord twanged through the air. Energy surged up her arm and gathered in her chest. Her pulse thundered in her veins. She closed her eyes, opened her mouth, and sang, letting the guitar give voice to her innermost hopes and dreams.

She effortlessly transitioned to a popular folk song about sorrowful ghosts and huge skies and wide desert wastes.

Her music was infectious. She could hear people tapping their feet and clapping, then a few began to sing along, then a few more, and a few more, until the song filled the entire theater. Marceline held the final note, both with her voice and the guitar, then slowly let it fade down into nothingness. She smiled and hummed, preparing to segue into a song she'd written a year ago about the salt waves crashing against the Salt Sea's shores. As she launched into the first arpeggio, she noticed something curious. The stage was vibrating. At first she thought it was her imagination. Then the vibrations grew more and more intense.

"Earthquake!" someone in the audience shouted. BMO snapped off the spotlight and brought up the houselights on a scene of utter pandemonium as people raced for the exit. Marceline fell back a step in confusion. When had there ever been an earthquake in Dustbowl City?

"Marceline!"

She whipped around and caught Bonnie as the other girl stumbled and fell against her.

"Are you all right?" Bonnie asked.

"What's going on?"

"I don't know—"

"Marceline!" BMO sprinted toward them as fast as its pipe-cleaner legs would allow. It kept close to the wall to avoid the crush of people. "We should get out of here now! People outside are saying something about a stampede of wild Lumpy Space Cows headed straight for town!"

The vibrations grew into a constant low rumbling.

"What?" Marceline slung her guitar strap over her shoulder. She thought she must have heard wrong. "What the shmoo are Lumpy Space Cows?"

Bonnie scowled. "The mayor leased a bunch of pastureland to some Lumpy Space King and Queen." She had to shout over the rumbling. "Something about their daughter's personal herd of specialty moo-cows."

"I really do think we should be leaving to find some higher ground now," BMO interjected.

"Let's go out the back." Bonnie tugged at Marceline's arm. Marceline scooped up BMO with her free hand as they ducked backstage.

Outside the theater's thick walls, the rumbling was so loud that Marceline could barely hear herself think. "Where should we go?" she shouted.

"Head to the big hill on the east side of town. I bet that's what everyone will do—you'll be safer with them."

"Aren't you coming?" Marceline yelled.

"I need to make sure the hotel is safe. I'll meet you there," said Bonnie, tugging Marceline through the theater's back alley.

On Sage Street, they joined a flood of townspeople. Bonnie was right—everyone had the same idea. Marceline caught sight of Jasper, flanked by Jake and Finn, frantically directing people. No one seemed to be paying much attention to them. As she watched, an old lady tripped and went down in the crowd, and Jasper lunged forward and fished her out. As he pulled her to her feet and shoved her behind him, he scanned the crowd again and spotted Marceline. For a split second they locked eyes. Jasper's were full of desperation.

Without thinking about it, Marceline tugged her hand free from Bonnie's grip.

Bonnie's head whipped around in shock, her braid slapping against her shoulder. "What are you doing? You've got to get out of here!"

"Jasper needs help," she said. "I'm going to stay." Before she could rethink it, she shoved BMO and her guitar into Bonnie's arms. "We'll meet you at the hill. Don't worry."

Marceline turned away and flexed her powers, using them to create space between each person in the crowd, keeping people from bumping into each other, from stepping on one another's heels, from tripping over their own feet. A hard line of pain formed above her right eye. She'd never used her power to control so many things at once before. Frowning in concentration, she shoved people forward, toward the hill. When they reached a place where the street widened enough that they were no longer in danger of crushing one another, she let them go. Everyone looked a little dazed, but luckily the general panic seemed to have defused. They climbed the hill, moving in quick but orderly lines, taking care to help the weak, slow, and aged.

"Do you think you can do that again?" Jasper asked as she dashed toward him. Sweat slid down the sides of his face and stained the underarms of his shirt. The ground shook, and the windows of the surrounding buildings rattled in their frames.

"I don't know." Her head throbbed. "Why?"

"Right now there's a herd of ticked-off Lumpy Space Cows headed straight for town. Maybe you could divert them."

Marceline frowned as she felt internal barriers slam into place. It was one thing to help people she'd grown up knowing, people she'd cared about at one time—people who maybe possibly still cared a little about her—but doing more than that? Stretching her power further than she'd ever tried before, further than might be possible . . . What if she hurt herself, what if she fried out the part of her head meat that let her use her power?

Her gaze roamed the street and came to a stop on one of the gas streetlamps. It sparked an idea.

She didn't need telekinesis to keep a bunch of cows from destroying Dustbowl.

She needed fire.

CHAPTER 14

"I told you to put the sword away! And hurry up! They're just over the next rise!"

"I don't see why we have to do what *she* says," Jake grumbled, making sure to pitch his voice loud enough to be heard over the omnipresent rumbling, as he and Finn dragged a huge tumbleweed out of a ditch.

"Because her idea might actually work!" Jasper snapped. He threw a tumbleweed of his own onto the huge pile they'd gathered in the center of Sutter Street. "Is this enough?"

Marceline nodded tightly and focused her

attention on the mound. "Stand back."

It just took a tiny spark. The tumbleweeds were dry as paper. Even though she was expecting it, the speed with which the weeds caught fire surprised her. She took a step back as the sudden heat bathed her cheeks.

"Do you think this'll work?" Jasper asked.

"If it doesn't, nothing will." She thought of the sand demons, all those years ago. "Everything's afraid of fire."

The four of them scrambled back, ducked around the corner of the closest building, and watched.

It wasn't just the rumbling that signaled the Lumpy Space Cows' arrival. Their thunderous lowing filled the air as they came over the rise and ran in a solid, lumpy line up the road toward them.

Deputy Finn winced and covered his ears. "Do you think this'll work?" he shouted.

"I ALREADY SAID YES!" Marceline screamed back.

"WHAT?"

Marceline snarled in annoyance and slapped her hand across Finn's mouth. Her eyes were fixed on the advancing line of cattle. They were huge—easily five or six times the size of a regular cow—purple, and covered in lumps. This close, she could see how red and rolling their eyes were, the spittle falling from their lips. Something had thoroughly spooked them. Suddenly she doubted the fire would be enough to deter them. From the way Jasper's knuckles whitened as he gripped the side of the building, his thoughts were probably traveling along similar lines.

Fifty feet away. Twenty. Ten. The lowing, the stamp of their hooves: It all merged into a huge roar that battered Marceline's senses mercilessly. The first animals reached the fire.

They turned.

Marceline released her pent-up breath. The cattle turned from the fire and headed out across the open plain to their left.

Gross warm wetness covered her palm, and she jerked her hand back in disgust. Finn had licked her!

"Keep your hand off my mouth!" he snapped.

"Ugh." Marceline wiped her hand on her pant leg. "Quit messing around!"

The majority of the cattle had detoured, following their herd leaders. There were five toward the back, though, who were either more frightened or more focused than the rest of the cattle. They headed straight up Sutter Street.

"No!" Jasper whipped his hat off his head and made as if he was going to run out in front of them.

Marceline swore and snatched at the back of his vest, almost dumping him onto his butt.

"What are you doing?" she yelled, pressing him back against the side of the building as the animals lumbered past. "You don't risk your life for a bunch of stupid buildings!"

"You're right."

The last animal disappeared up the street. A few seconds later, there was a huge crashing and snapping.

Marceline yelped as Deputy Jake's head stretched out around the buildings. "I didn't know he could do that!"

Jasper grinned. "He's multitalented. I didn't hire him for no good reason."

"They're going straight through the hotel!" Jake said. Finn scrambled up on Jake's shoulders and then shinnied up his neck to get a better view. Marceline froze at the sound of breaking wood. Was Bonnie okay?

"And through the general store!" Finn reported.

Jake's neck stretched a little higher. "Looks like they're taking out the bank, too."

"Oh glob," Jasper groaned. "I'll never hear the end of this from the mayor. He's gonna take all the repair costs right out of my budget."

CHAPTER 15

Bonnie joined them as they stood next to the wreckage of the Old Town Hotel. BMO toddled beside her. The Lumpy Space Cattle had finally run themselves to exhaustion, and the Lumpy Space King and Queen had sent servants to round them up and return them to their pasture.

"Everyone safe?" Jasper asked.

Bonnie handed Marceline her guitar. "Mrs. Evans twisted her ankle, but everyone else is fine."

"Miss Bubblegum, I think you're going to need to find a new job," BMO said.

Marceline snorted. "That's an understatement."

"At least nobody was seriously hurt," Jake said.

"Yeah! Focus on the positive! Mathematical!" Finn unsheathed his sword and struck a pose, flexing his biceps.

"Sheriff Sterling! I need to talk to you now!" Mayor Starchy stamped up to Jasper.

"Mayor." Jasper swallowed. "I know it looks bad, but believe me, it would be much worse if—"

"The bank, Sheriff! The bank's been wiped out!"

Jake nodded sagely. "That makes sense. It is right behind the general store."

"No!" Mayor Starchy exclaimed. "The building's fine! It's the money! The money's all gone!"

"I knew it!" Jake leaped forward, sticking his finger in Marceline's face. "She did it—she's behind this somehow! Once a thief, always a thief!"

CHAPTER 16

Jail cells had a peculiar smell. Marceline hadn't really noticed it the first time she'd sat in one. Now, however, she wondered how she'd missed it. A little like a mixture of sweaty socks and cinnamon.

"I'm telling you, you're wrong!" Bonnie's voice carried clearly down the hall that connected the front of the jail to the back room where the cells were. "She can't have done it. The whole town saw her; she went straight from the stage to the center of town. She was even *helping* the sheriff!"

Marceline leaned her head back against the wall and closed her eyes. "Just give it a rest, Bonnie!"

she shouted. The fact that she could still hear the mayor ranting and raving didn't give her much hope anyone would be listening to Bonnie any time soon. She picked at the cold-steel collar Mayor Starchy had insisted on slapping around her neck. Whatever. She was an old hand at all this now. Hardened. She gargled until she had the makings of a good spitball, took careful aim, and spat. She got good height on it. It splattered satisfyingly against the ceiling.

"Just let me go back and see her for a minute!"

Marceline looked over as Bonnie skidded to a stop outside her cell. The other girl's cheeks were flushed, and tears gleamed in her eyes.

"Marcy," she said urgently, her voice low. "Jasper knows you couldn't have done it. He'll get them to listen to reason. We just need to get the mayor to calm down."

"Where is she? Where's our daughter?"

Bonnie and Marceline locked eyes. They both

knew that voice: Pa Bubblegum. A moment later, both Ma and Pa appeared behind Bonnie, followed closely by Jake and the sheriff.

"That's enough, sweetheart," Ma said, pulling Bonnie away from the cell.

Bonnie shook her head. "Ma, no—"

"I'm not surprised she's speaking up for her friend," Jake interjected in a deceptively calm drawl. He leaned against the door to the cellblock and glared at Bonnie through half-lidded eyes. "They're probably in cahoots."

Ma and Pa both paled. "Sheriff Sterling." Pa's eyes sparked with anger. "You tell your man to watch his slanderous mouth."

"Deputy." Jasper's voice was sharp. "Out. Now."

"But, Sheriff!"

"Now. Take Deputy the Human and go process the crime scene."

Later, after everyone had huffed off in various stages of disgruntlement, Jasper dragged a chair into the back. Heaving a sigh, he collapsed into the chair and dropped his head into his hands.

"You know I don't think you did it," he said.

Marceline stared up at the ceiling. "Sounds like you and Bonnie are the only ones."

"We'll find out what really happened."

"Is my guitar okay?"

"It's fine. BMO's sitting on it."

"Where?"

"At my house. And when I say 'sitting on it,' I mean that literally. It's sitting *on* the case."

She smiled. "BMO takes its job super seriously." Despite everything that had happened that day, she surprised herself with a yawn.

"Want some coffee?"

Marceline's smile widened. "Real coffee, or Dustbowl City coffee?"

"If you mean, do I have a can that has about two teaspoons' worth of ground-up coffee beans mixed with a whole lot of chicory, then yes, it's authentic Dustbowl City coffee."

"Some things never change."

With a groan, Jasper pushed himself to his feet. "I'll put the kettle on."

Marceline folded her arms behind her head. "They didn't even look at me."

He paused in the doorway. "I know."

Marceline horked another spitball. This one fell short and landed back on the cot. *Oh well.*

"Jake, wait, this doesn't feel very algebraic. We should think about this—" It was Finn's voice, raised in high-pitched tones of panic.

"We've done enough waiting and thinking! I'm done thinking! Thinking's gotten us nowhere!"

Marceline sat up on the cot. They sounded like they were right outside her tiny barred window. She and Jasper exchanged a quick glance. There was a scuffle of receding footsteps as they walked around the side of the building. A few seconds later, the jail's front door banged open.

"You!" Jake, quivering with anger, lurched into the cellblock. A maroon folder was tucked under his arm. He stretched a trembling finger toward Jasper. "I should've guessed. This whole situation's been hinky from day one."

"Whoa." Jasper held up his hands. "What're you talking about?"

"It's all here." Jake slapped the folder against Jasper's chest. Papers slipped out and scattered across the floor. "You let her go the first time!"

CHAPTER 17

"I took a little side trip to the City Hall annexed basement back-room storage closet. It's got a letter from the warden of the quarry prison saying Marceline never showed up to serve her time! I don't have to be a genius to read between the lines and figure out what really happened."

Marceline slapped her forehead in disbelief. "Why would you keep something that incriminating?"

"Well, who'd think someone would ever find it down there?" Jasper squawked. "Dad was a bit compulsive when it came to paperwork."

"You belong in there with her!" Jake stretched out

his arms and wrapped them around Jasper, pinning his arms to his sides. "Finn, get that cell door open."

Moving with obvious reluctance, Finn stepped past Jake, key in hand.

Marceline kicked the bars in frustration. "You guys are making a big mistake."

"Of course you'd say that," Jake snarled. "You're in cahoots. And I'll find a way to prove Bonnie's in on it, too."

"Jake, I dunno about this," Finn said. "Jasper's always been great to work for. So what if he made a mistake five years ago?"

Jake squinted long and hard at Finn. "That sounds like cahoots talk, Finn. You want me to start wonderin' if you're a cahooter, too?"

Finn's eyes widened. "Nope, not at all, not even a little tiny bit, whatever you say, Deputy-Sheriff." He unlocked the cell and swung the door open. Jake stuffed Jasper into the cell and slammed the door shut.

"Right." He dusted off his paws and glanced at Finn. "I'll stand guard, you run and get the mayor. We'll settle this right now." He glared at Marceline. "And you better think about telling me what you did with all the money you stole from the bank."

"Oh my glob." Marceline banged her head against the bars. "I can't believe I came back here."

And that was when the wall behind Jake and Finn exploded. None of them had any time to react as a huge bang simultaneously deafened them and knocked them off their feet. The noise and pressure shattered Marceline's mind, and when she came to, she was lying on her back, staring at the ceiling. Her ears rang. A thin, black-masked figure loomed over her.

"Get up," the figure murmured. She couldn't tell if it was male or female. It prodded her with the toe of its boot. "Get up."

She groaned and sat up. Something dropped

off her face and landed on her lap. Something wet and squishy. She looked down. A scrap of torn pink vegetable matter. She became aware of its smell.

Overripe watermelon. The whole room was covered in it. Now that she was aware of it, the smell was overwhelming.

A second, similarly dressed figure joined the first. They each grabbed one of Marceline's arms and hauled her up.

Her legs didn't want to support her. She caught a quick glimpse of Jasper lying a few feet away, and Jake and Finn, flat on their faces, their limbs splayed like a dead lizard's. "Jasper." It came out slurred.

"Be quiet," one of the intruders said. They hustled her out of the cell. She couldn't help them much. Her feet kept tangling on chunks of splintered wood and slipping on watermelon pulp. She blinked and shook her head, trying to clear it.

"Who are you?" she managed.

Neither person answered her. They dragged her out through the hole in the jail wall, toward a pair of waiting horses. The cold night air helped to clear Marceline's head. She heard shouts and the sound of people running. The intruders tied her hands behind her with what felt like a length of incredibly cheap, scratchy rope and tossed her up onto one of the horses. One of the intruders swung up behind her. The next thing she knew, they were racing toward the outskirts of town.

She couldn't decide if her situation had just gotten better or worse.

CHAPTER 18

The intruders reined in their horses a few miles outside of town, near a wind-smoothed sandstone outcropping.

"Are you guys fans?" Marceline asked as the riders dismounted. Neither replied. She frowned. "Look, I'm sure you think you're doing me a favor, but I don't see how this is going to make me look less suspicious."

The taller of the two figures reached up and pulled her from the saddle. She landed on his shoulder, and a familiar scent of hard work, berry stew, and hay filled her nostrils.

"Pa?" she whispered. The figure stiffened and slowly set her down on her feet. After a moment's hesitation, he reached up and pulled off his mask.

"Pa." She stared up into his tired eyes. Wearily, he scrubbed his stubbly cheek with the palm of his hand. The second person moved to stand beside him and took off her hood, as well. Ma's equally tired eyes stared out at her from beneath her mussed, gray-streaked hair.

"Marceline," she said, her voice cool. She pushed a lock of hair back behind her ear.

"Long time no see," Marceline said. Up close, they looked small and old and gray. "You want an autograph or something?"

Pa Bubblegum drew a knife from his belt and cut through the ropes they'd used to tie her hands.

Ma Bubblegum took a step forward. "We want you to leave," she said, curling her right hand into a fist and pressing it over her heart. "Just go. Tonight."

Marceline guffawed. "Leave? Just run off and let everyone think I was behind that bank robbery?" She flushed with anger. "Forget it."

Pa held his hand out toward her in a warding gesture. "We don't want trouble."

"Please, think of Bonnie." Ma's eyes were bright. "You've been able to start your life over, but her reputation's suffered. It took years for people to stop treating her weird, and now all that talk's starting up again. Please, if you care about her at all, just go."

"No way." Marceline shook her head. "I can admit that I was totally guilty of that train heist, but I had nothing to do with this bank thing. No way I'm going to let Jake be all filled with smugness, thinking he's right. No flooping way. I'm going to stay here and help Jasper clear my name, and then I'm going to write an awesome song about it."

Pa's mouth tightened. "We'll pay you."

Marceline gave him a doubtful look. The harvest

couldn't have improved *that* much over the years.

"That's enough, Pa," Bonnie said as she stepped out from behind a boulder.

Ma and Pa gasped.

"How'd you find us?" Ma asked.

Bonnie shot her mother a scornful look. "You guys aren't exactly subtle. You used sweet grenade watermelons to blow up the jail! Who else grows those things around here? And you didn't even try to hide your horses' tracks." Her gaze flicked to Marceline. "You okay?"

"Yeah," Marceline said dazedly.

"Bonnie, you be a good girl and head on home," Pa said. "This isn't any of your concern."

Bonnie's eyes flashed. "How is your trying to pay Marceline to leave town none of my concern?"

"Honey, please," Ma said. "We're just looking out for you."

"Oh." Bonnie arched an eyebrow. "Like last time?"

Pa's face flushed an ugly red, and Ma said, "Bonnie, please!"

"All four of you, freeze!" For the second time that evening, an unexpected voice rang out. This time, it belonged to Jasper. He stepped out from behind the outcropping, his hands wrapped around a weapon Marceline recognized as the make-you-forget-how-to-run gun his father had shot her with on that day five years ago.

"Mr. and Mrs. Bubblegum?" Jasper did a double take that would have been amusing under other circumstances and holstered his weapon. "I hope you have an explanation for this. Because I have to tell you, this situation doesn't look good."

"Jasper, you only need to know one thing." Bonnie tossed her pink braid over her shoulder. "I'm the one who robbed the bank."

CHAPTER 19

Except for the dull whisper of the wind, it was so silent that Marceline thought she probably could have heard a gumball drop.

"Excuse me?" Jasper finally managed.

"Bonnie, c'mon." Marceline gripped the other girl's arm. "I get you want to help me out, but really, this isn't the way to do it."

"Marceline." Bonnie turned and met Marceline's gaze. Something in Marceline's stomach twisted, because she saw dead seriousness in her friend's eyes. "I'm not kidding. I did it. I used your old trick, panic grass, to spook the herd and get them to stampede."

Her gaze flicked to Jasper. "I'd have come clean sooner, but I didn't think you'd arrest Marceline, since she was with you the whole time. I wanted to do another robbery to clear her name. But I don't think that's necessary now. The money's not far from here. I can show you where I hid it." Bonnie held out her wrists. "Go ahead and arrest me."

"She's lying!" Ma Bubblegum darted forward.

Bonnie shook her head. "Ma, Pa, it's over. You can't help me this time. There's no way you can make something this big go away."

Cold trailed down Marceline's spine.

"Bonnie, please, don't say any more," Pa begged tearfully.

"I've lived with the guilt for five years. I don't want to deal with it any longer. My parents paid off the judge at our trial. That's why he let me go."

"What are you talking about?" said Marceline. "We barely had enough money for food back then.

How was there enough for a bribe?"

"Well, of course we had a reserve fund for Bonnie's future," said Pa, looking scornfully at Marceline. "But there was no reason for either of you to know about it then—or now, for that matter. We were just doing what we could to look out for our own daughter."

Marceline's heart plummeted. Part of her couldn't believe what they had said was true, but another part wasn't the least bit surprised. She remembered the hateful look Ma had given her that awful day in the courtroom. Almost immediately, guilt stabbed at her. Bonnie didn't know that she hadn't served her time. She'd spent five years tormenting herself for no reason.

"You were such a bad influence on her!" Ma yelled at Marceline. "You dragged her into that heist! She never would have done it on her own."

"Ma, how many times do I have to tell you that's not true?" Bonnie's face reddened. "I wasn't some innocent little gumdrop."

"What the cabbage is going on here?"

Marceline stifled a groan. Just what they needed: *another* newcomer added into the increasingly turgid drama. To her surprise, not just one or two but *three* people joined them: Judge Ice King, wearing a dusty traveling coat and hat, flanked by Jake and Finn.

"Glob, I knew it!" Jake cried. "She and Bonnie *are* in cahoots!"

"Vindication!" Finn swung his sword off his back and struck a pose. "Mathematical!"

Judge Ice King glanced at Jasper. "I got here as soon as I received your deputies' telegram regarding the stampede and bank theft." At the mention of the telegram, Jasper glared at Jake, who looked back solemnly. Judge Ice King placed his fists on his scrawny hips. "Up to trouble again, Miss Abadeer? Yes, I remember you. And young Miss Bubblegum."

"Judge Ice King." Pa Bubblegum's face was ashen. "I'm sure we can work this out."

"No!" Bonnie shouted. "I'm not going to let you do this again!" Quick as a flash, she reached into the pocket of her gingham dress, pulled out a small, clear green ball, and threw it on the ground. The ball made a sound like pudding striking a wall. It flattened like a lump of clay, and then tendrils shot outward, wrapping around Bonnie. The translucent mint-green stuff encased her entire body except for her face. Bonnie clenched her left hand into a fist, and sparks surrounded it. Everyone gasped and fell back.

"What the glob is that stuff?" Finn exclaimed.

Jasper pulled out his weapon. "Bonnie, what are you thinking about doing?"

"Yeah." Marceline tried to sound glib, even though she could feel sweat seeping through her clothes. "Come on, let's sit down and talk about all this. Did you make that stuff? It's pretty cool. Why don't you tell me how it works?"

Bonnie rolled her eyes. "Oh, come on, Marcy. You

really think I'm going to fall for that?"

She lifted her right arm and pointed at Judge Ice King, and the gel darted toward him like a fat, impossibly quick slug. Jasper swore, and blobby yellow light blorped from the mouth of his gun—Marceline had to admit it looked pretty cool—but the blast of energy pinged harmlessly off Bonnie's gel armor. The gel tendril wrapped around Judge Ice King. Bonnie flicked her wrist, and the gel retracted, yanking the judge to her side. She held him, dangling, a few feet off the ground. He bristled. "Hey now! This is unbelievably rude and all kinds of illegal!"

"Oh, be quiet." Bonnie's gel covered the judge's mouth, silencing him. His eyes bulged with shock and rage. "Hey, not so fast," she said, and Marceline realized that Jake was stretching his arms toward Bonnie. Jake grasped Bonnie's ankles and tried to snatch her off her feet. Bonnie leaped back nimbly, swung her other hand, and knocked Jake down.

"Hey, no fair! This has gotta be some kind of cheating," Jake spluttered as a puddle of gel detached from Bonnie's armor and pinned him to the ground like a bug.

"Bonnie, what are you doing?" Tears ran down Ma's cheeks. "Please think about this! Think about your future!"

"That's all I've done for the last five years!" Bonnie shouted back. "I know what my future *should* have been, but you guys interfered and left Marcy out in the cold. We should have served the same amount of time together."

"We just wanted to help you," Pa said. "You're our daughter."

Bonnie's face was cold. "You're such hypocrites."

"Bonnie, come on." Marceline inched toward Bonnie, hoping there was some way she could tear Judge Ice King free of that weird, grasping gel stuff. "If anyone should feel bummed about all this, it's me, and even I think you're being kind of harsh. I can admit I wasn't an easy kid to love, what with all the messes and the fires and that time I dropped a tree on the house—which I hope you two remember was totally an accident." She stared pointedly at Ma and Pa before continuing.

"Don't make excuses for them!" The gel around Bonnie's legs suddenly stretched, shooting her up ten feet into the air. "Jasper, if you want the judge back, you're going to have to arrest me." The judge tight in her grasp, Bonnie walked as if on stilts and quickly disappeared from sight.

"I'd just like to take a moment to remind everyone how right I was," Jake piped up.

CHAPTER 20

Marceline, Jasper, and Finn pulled on Jake's arms, trying to free him from the gel. Behind them, Ma and Pa held each other and cried.

"Come on, guys!" Jake whined. "Get me outta here. This stuff is gross."

"Ugh, it really doesn't want to let go," Marceline said. "Finn, do you think you can cut through it with your sword?"

Finn eyed it appraisingly. "I can try." He stuck the point of his sword into the gel. The blade cut through the gel cleanly, as if it were butter.

"Hey! Watch it!"

"Whoops! Sorry."

The gel tried to seal itself almost as soon as Finn sliced it. Marceline and Jasper yanked again, hard, on Jake's arms. He broke free with an audible pop.

"Whew, that stuff is disgusting." He shook himself hard until his fur stuck out in all directions. He peered up at Marceline. "Did you know she had something like that?"

"*Puh-lease*. When I knew her, she was working on fixing watches and making unipolarity generators."

Jasper pushed back his hat and scratched his head. "Looks like she's picked up a few tricks since then."

Finn carefully wiped the blade of his sword on his shirt before he sheathed it. "What do we do now?"

Ma Bubblegum blew her nose loudly into her handkerchief. "Please don't hurt her."

Marceline and Jasper exchanged a glance.

"We've got to convince her to let the judge go," Jasper said quietly.

Jake scowled. "That means we've gotta find her first. Did any of you see which way she went?"

"No."

"Nope."

"Nuh-uh."

They all froze as they heard footsteps.

"Marceline?" BMO tottered around the side of the outcropping. "There you are! It's a good thing those nice people who blew up the jail and kidnapped you left such a clear and easy trail to follow. Your friend Bonnie passed me a little while ago. She was very much green and seemed to be very tall all of a sudden."

Marceline knelt beside BMO. "Did you see where she was going?"

BMO cocked its head to one side. "She was heading back toward town."

"Oh man." Marceline slapped her forehead. "I think I know what she's got in mind."

Jake and Finn stared at her. "What?" Finn asked breathlessly.

"She doesn't want anyone to be able to cover this up, right?"

Jasper's eyes widened. "Downtown. She'll take the judge downtown."

Marceline nodded. "And she'll make sure everyone sees that she's got him. Then there's no way he can let her off."

"And he's not going to want to risk people finding out that he took a bribe."

She nodded again. "It would ruin his reputation. He'd probably lose his position, maybe even end up in jail himself."

"And how are we supposed to stop her?" Finn asked. "That suit of hers is pretty amazing."

"Ooh!" Jake hopped up and down in excitement. "I could make my arms into a giant slingshot, and we could lob boulders at her!"

Marceline smacked him upside the back of his head. "We're not going to hurt her."

Jake sniffed. "Who says I have to listen to you?"

"I do," Jasper said. "As of now, I'm deputizing her. And I'm making her a . . . um . . . silver manatee lumberjack deputy. Which makes her your superior." As if to underline his statement, Jasper walked behind Marceline and unlocked the magic-deadening collar.

"*Awww!* I wanna be a silver manatee lumberjack!" Finn said.

"Maybe tomorrow. If you're good."

"Glob! Is this all settled?" Marceline looked pointedly from one to the other. "Okay, good. We don't need to worry about the suit. All we have to do is free Judge Ice King."

CHAPTER 21

They ran along the side of the remaining buildings in single file, keeping low to the ground. As Marceline had guessed, Bonnie was indeed holding the judge captive in town—on top of the bank. The sun was just rising, and Bonnie stood with her back to it, her gel suit perfectly outlined by the strengthening golden rays, wreathing her in the illusion of liquid flames. Judge Ice King, still gagged, sat beside her on the peaked roof, the upper portion of his face furrowed in a pout so fierce, a toddler would have been hard-pressed to top it.

The bank was the oldest and fanciest building

in all of Dustbowl. It was made of thick blocks of cut gray stone, making it seem as though Bonnie were standing atop a castle.

They ducked down behind a pile of rubble. A crowd of townspeople had gathered. They stared up at Bonnie. She shouted something Marceline couldn't make out, then flung something over the crowd, something that flashed silver and gold, and pattered against the ground like fat hailstones. People cried out, first in fear, then in excitement, and began scuttling around on the ground after the things.

"Money!" Jake exclaimed. "She's throwing down money from the bank heist!"

Finn gasped and, a huge grin on his face, darted forward, his eyes wibbling and glistening with excitement.

"Finn!" Jake's arms stretched out, tripped up Finn before he could give away their position, and dragged him back behind the rubble.

"But money, Jake!"

"It's stolen!" Jake hissed. "You wouldn't be able to keep it. *Yeesh.*"

"Wait here," Marceline whispered. "I'm gonna try to talk her down."

Jasper nodded, and he and Jake sat very pointedly on Finn.

She took a deep breath and stepped into sight. "Hey, Bonnie," she called. "How ya doing up there?"

"Just fine," Bonnie shouted back.

Marceline shoved her hands into her pockets and teetered back and forth on her heels. "Shaping up to be a nice day."

"What do you want, Marcy?"

"I was just thinking, it's probably going to be hot today. You maybe want to let Judge Ice King go, come on down, maybe get some lemonade and talk things over?"

The judge's eyes widened, and he nodded his head frantically.

Bonnie ignored her. "Is Jasper with you?"

"Yeah."

"Tell him to come out." She shook Judge Ice King for emphasis until his stiff whiskers rattled.

"I'm here." Jasper moved into the open.

"I want you to get Mayor Starchy and bring him here. I'm not coming down until someone makes me some solid assurances that I'm going to jail."

"Like a contract?" Finn shouted from behind the rubble.

"Yes! That's what I want! You and the mayor go draft a contract!"

"That makes sense to me," Jake called. "Write in that you're locking her up for a bajillion years."

"Well, I dunno," Jasper said, rubbing the back of his neck. "It may take me quite a while to find the mayor."

"Assistant Mayor Lemongrab is hiding under that bench over there!"

Marceline dropped her face into her hand with a groan.

"Thanks, Finn," Jasper said through gritted teeth. "You're a big help."

"He's also a notary public!"

Jake's arms stretched out from behind the rubble, grabbed Lemongrab, and dragged him out from under the bench. The assistant mayor screamed a series of jumbled words and left fingernail marks in the dirt. Jake dumped him unceremoniously next to Jasper.

As soon as he hit the ground, Lemongrab stopped screaming. He stood and, with as much dignity as he could muster, dusted off his clothes.

"How many years would you like to be in jail for?" he shrieked up at Bonnie. He pulled a pad of paper out of one pocket and a surprisingly large silver stamp out of the other.

Bonnie's eyes widened. "Gosh, I didn't really think I'd get to pick."

"Bonnie, we need to talk now!" Marceline yelled.

"Wait!"

Everyone's heads whipped around in time to see Ma and Pa Bubblegum, trailing a bemused BMO, as they raced toward the bank. It was Ma Bubblegum who had called out. They screeched to a halt in front of Lemongrab.

"Assistant Mayor," Ma managed between gasps. "Please, my daughter's not feeling well."

"Don't listen to anything she says." Pa gripped Lemongrab's shoulders and shook him. "She's very, very ill. She needs a doctor. And a whopping big shot of laudanum."

"Oh my glob! Ma, Pa, I've had it with you interfering in my life!" Bonnie threw two shining red baubles at her parents. They struck the ground inches from their feet and splashed outward, growing into huge mounds of gummy pink froth that wrapped around her parents and froze them in place.

Townspeople screamed and scattered.

"Hey now!" Jake hopped out from behind the rubble and stretched his arms toward Bonnie. Bonnie's mouth twisted, and she threw another glob of slime at Jake, pinning him to a nearby public message board.

"Oh. Yeah." Jake stared dazedly at the gel. "This stuff again."

Bonnie raised a yellow sphere and waggled it threateningly at Lemongrab. "You! Start working on that contract." Lemongrab swallowed so hard, he almost ate his Adam's apple. He dropped to his knees in the dirt and started scribbling frantically in his notebook.

"Okay!" Marceline held her hands out. "Before things get any more totally out of control. Bonnie. You and I need to talk. Now."

"There's nothing you can say, Marcy."

"Bonnie—"

"I can't live with this guilt any longer."

"BONNIE—"

"One way or another, I'm going to make sure I'm brought to justice."

"BONNIE! I NEVER SERVED MY TIME!"

Bonnie's jaw dropped. For a moment, Marceline worried her eyes were going to pop out of her head.

"Wh-what?" Bonnie squeaked.

Marceline shot a quick warning glance at Jasper. "I tricked Jasper into taking off my chains, and I ran away. I've been traveling around the country playing ever since."

"B-but . . ."

"Marceline, is this true?" BMO trilled. Fat tears squeezed out of its eye pixels. "Are you not Billy, after all? I love you anyway, but this is a very depressing revelation."

"I know, I'm the worst. But, Bonnie, I had no idea you were planning all this."

"Bonnie!" Jasper shouted. "Please, let the judge go. There's no reason for you to throw away your life like this. Marcy's sentence was totally bogus anyway! I can write a letter to an appellate court or, at the very least, a less crappity judge. We can work this out."

Huge tears wobbled in Bonnie's eyes. They spilled down her cheeks and splashed on the slate shingles. Her expression tugged at Marceline's heart. Powerful emotions flooded her chest with warmth, and that warmth spread into her limbs and lifted her into the air. Shock filled her—she'd tried, off and on over the years, to use her power to fly, but every attempt had left her shaking, exhausted, and stubbornly earthbound. She floated effortlessly up toward Bonnie, feeling as if she were watching herself from across the room. When she was level with the other girl, she held out her hands and grasped Bonnie's shoulders.

"Bonnie," she said softly. "I was going to tell Finn to cut through your suit with his sword to free Judge

Ice King. But it'll be better if you do it yourself."

"All those years . . ." Bonnie's lip quivered. "All those nights I went to sleep hating myself . . ."

"I'm so sorry." Tears burned Marceline's eyes. "I should have sent you a letter, but I was afraid of getting caught again . . . and I was too busy being mad at everyone in Dustbowl."

"Oh, Marcy . . ." Bonnie tapped on the front of her suit, and the gel rippled off her body and puddled around her feet. Judge Ice King fell onto the roof with a squawk. Jake reached up and pulled the man to safety while Bonnie threw her arms around Marceline and hugged her.

Marceline hugged her back. "We sure turned out to be a pair of screwups."

Bonnie laughed, shakily, into her ear.

"Um . . . sorry about this."

They heard the sound of steel clinking. Bonnie and Marceline turned. Finn, held aloft by Jake, had slapped a handcuff around one of Bonnie's wrists. Before she could react, Finn snapped the other cuff around Marceline's wrist.

He shrugged apologetically. "You guys *have* broken, like, a ton of laws."

CHAPTER 22

"Well," Marceline said with a sigh, "here we go again."

"This situation does rate pretty high on a general scale of suckitude," Bonnie said.

"Both of you, shut up!" Judge Ice King scowled down at them from the bench.

Marceline rolled her eyes, picked at the anti-magic collar Jake had snapped back around her neck, and heaved another dramatic sigh.

Unlike their first trial, this time Judge Ice King had ordered the proceedings to be closed. The gallery was empty. The only people other than Marceline and Bonnie that Judge Ice King had allowed in the courtroom were Jasper, Finn, and Jake. He'd insisted on holding the trial about three minutes after she had floated herself and Bonnie down from the bank.

Now he stood up behind the bench and leaned against it, his hair bristling around his head, his indignation palpable.

Jasper cleared his throat. "Judge, I think there are mitigating circumstances that you should perhaps take into consideration—"

"Yeah!" Jake interjected. "Like the fact you totally took a *bribe*."

As Judge Ice King's blue face turned a deep, deep mauve, Jasper coughed, loudly and repeatedly. "I was thinking more the mental pain and suffering Bonnie has dealt with over the years. I think a case can be made for diminished capacity—"

"Enough with your six-dollar words!" Judge Ice King hollered. "I have had it with you, and him"—

he pointed at Jake—"and her, and ESPECIALLY HER!!!" He jabbed his finger at Bonnie. With an enraged yowl, he threw his gavel across the room. "I hate being kidnapped! It's so inconsiderate! I can't believe such a cute girl is so awful!" He hauled himself up onto the bench and stamped his feet. "I'm super close to revoking your sheriffhood. What kind of idiot lawman lets a fourteen-year-old girl escape during a routine transfer?"

Jasper's face flushed.

"Shows what you know!" Jake shouted. "She didn't escape, Jas— OW! My feets!"

"Sorry." Finn shrugged. "I tripped."

"That's enough!" Judge Ice King hopped up and down. Spittle flew from his mouth. "I'm sentencing both of them to five years smashing rocks in that quarry I tried to send the first one to five years ago! And this time, you blorping well better make sure they actually get there!"

As soon as he finished talking, he glared at Marceline, as if daring her to repeat her previous freak-out.

Marceline stared back at him. Careful to keep her face expressionless, she hawked up the biggest, snottiest, spittiest loogie she'd ever hawked.

Then she spit it right on the hem of his robe.

Later, after Judge Ice King had finished screaming and crying and had stomped out of the courtroom with a final glower at Marceline and Bonnie, Jasper and the deputies led them out into the narrow alley that ran behind the courthouse. Bonnie's parents stood there waiting. When Bonnie emerged, they cried out and rushed toward her.

"Five years," Jasper said grimly. "For each of them."

Ma and Pa sobbed.

Bonnie hugged her parents. "Don't cry. Five

years isn't that long." She smiled bravely. "And who knows? Working in a quarry may turn out to be a valuable life skill."

"We're sorry," Ma said. "We made a mistake five years ago."

Pa turned toward Marceline. "We owe you an apology, too," he said gruffly. He wiped his eyes. "You were just girls. It was wrong of us to put all the blame on you."

A huge, genuine smile nearly split Marceline's face in half. "Thank you." She hugged him, hard, and then Bonnie pulled all four of them into a tight embrace.

CHAPTER 23

They left at dawn a few days later. Bonnie and Marceline had told Jasper not to tell Ma and Pa Bubblegum when they were leaving—they'd both agreed the good-bye would be too hard on their parents. They'd write as soon as possible. When she'd gone to sleep the night before, Marceline had overheard Bonnie and BMO talking excitedly about developing some kind of two-way radio interface using grasshoppers as transmitters.

Just past the edge of town, the small party reined in their horses.

"You gonna be okay here, on your own?" Jasper

asked Jake and Finn as they prepared to part.

Jake nodded. "I think so." He grunted as Finn dug an elbow into his ribs. "Oh yeah . . . before I forget, here." He handed Jasper a thick sheaf of papers in a folder bound with a piece of twine. "That's everything I could find about Marceline's original trial and you letting her go an' stuff. Your dad really was a freak for paperwork."

Jasper smiled at his deputy. "You sure you're okay with this?"

"Yeah. I've been taking things too seriously. Things are a lot more complicated than I used to think they were." He sighed wistfully. "I think maybe I'm going to focus on this pen pal thing I got going with a Lady Rainicorn."

"Well, that said, I hereby dub thee the new sheriff of Dustbowl City." Jasper unpinned his badge and handed it to Jake. He glanced at Finn. "Don't let the power go to his head."

"Yes, sir!" Finn's smile dimmed. "You guys really will write, right?"

"Of course we will," Bonnie said. "And as soon as we get the ticket sales from our first concert, we'll send you guys a check to cover all the damage I did to town."

Marceline groaned. Bonnie glanced at her sharply. "It's only right," she said.

"Yeah, I know," Marceline sighed. Scowling, she focused on the folder. A wisp of smoke rose from a blackening corner before it burst into flames. Jasper yelped and dropped it. Marceline grinned impishly. "Sorry."

BMO frowned. "That was not nice, Marceline."

"I said sorry."

Jasper heaved a sigh. "I can see you're going to keep me on my toes."

"You don't have to come with us," Marceline said. "You can stay here."

Jasper shook his head. "I'm like Jake. I've changed. A life of service ain't what it used to be. I want to travel. Take a little me time."

"Good," BMO said. "A second road manager will be most welcome."

With a last wave good-bye, Marceline, Bonnie, Jasper, and BMO headed off into the west. It would have been more poetic, Marceline mused, if they'd been riding into a sunset instead of away from a sunrise, but she supposed you couldn't have everything.

About the Author

The elusive T. T. MacDangereuse is one of the most popular authors in all of Ooo. Although little is known about her private life, it is rumored that she learned the art of storyship at a very young age after being rescued from a pack of jitter-bugging party bears by The Prince of the Pencil Kingdom. She claims that all her story ideas are inspired hallucinations caused by eating too many apple pies.